ARNE MELLOR

Erotic Romance
A COMMANDER'S Way

WARNING

This book contains sexually explicit scenes and adult language. It may be considered offensive to some readers. This book is for sale to adults ONLY.

* * * * * * * * * * * * * * * * * * *

Please store your files wisely where they cannot be accessed by underage readers.

Please feel free to send me an email. Just know that these emails are filtered by my publisher. Good news is always welcome.

Arne Mellor – **arne_mellor@awesomeauthors.org**

You might also want to check my blog for Updates and interesting info.
http://arne-mellor.awesomeauthors.org/

About the Publisher

BLVNP Incorporated, A Nevada Corporation, 340 S. Lemon #6200, Walnut CA 91789, info@blvnp.com / legal@blvnp.com
NOTE: Due to the highly emotional reaction of some people to works of erotic fiction any email sent to the above address that contains foul language or religious references is automatically deleted by our anti-spam software and will not be seen. All other communications are welcome.

DISCLAIMER

Please don't be stupid and kill yourself. This book is a work of FICTION. Do not try any new sexual practice that you find in this book. It is fiction and not to be confused with reality. Neither the author nor the publisher or its associates assume any responsibility for any loss, injury, death or legal consequences resulting from acting on the contents in this book. Every character in this book is over 18 years of age. The author's opinions are not to be construed as the opinions of the publisher. The material in this book is for entertainment purposes ONLY. Enjoy.

A Commander's Way

Erotic Romance

By: Arne Mellor

ISBN: 978-1-62761-749-9

DUKE Evan Frome, the newly appointed ruler of Gideon IV was tired. It had been an exhausting first day in the capital, with the clearing of the last pockets of Vordanian forces. There was a planet to rebuild, an army to reform, and Evan noted grimly, comrades to bury. But tonight at least he could at least enjoy the fruits of his desperate battles against the Vordanian occupation forces. Gideon was free again. And there was a celebration to attend.

He stopped by the mecha hangars before returning to the palace, taking reassurance from the familiar smells of fuel and heavy machinery and the constant hum of servos. The tech crews were already hard at work repairing and rearming the surviving warmechas, arc welders sending sprays of glittering sparks everywhere. Many of the techs greeted him by name, and Evan soon found his neck stiff from nodding in reply. He liked being with the troops. Here, one was appreciated for performance and ability, not merely who your father was. Evan took care to commend and reward those who had done well under his command and his engaging, down-to-earth manner made him popular with the troops. He shuddered at being called Duke Frome, preferring his military rank of Commander which was a title he had earned, not given as a birthright.

He found his battered Delta-class warmecha in one corner of the bustling hanger. The new kills from the last desperate battle inside the palace compound were already painted on the cockpit. Evan squinted as he studied the row of icons, noting that he was just one short of three dozen victories. Sometime during their battles, the loyalist forces had salvaged this unusual Vordanian chassis from a storage bunker in the desert. With its gaping beam weapon bays, the machine was for pilots who believed in firepower. Evan found that the design philosophy was a perfect match for the way he liked to fight and stuck with it throughout his remaining battles on Gideon. He walked around the massive 70-ton war machine, wincing at the jagged holes in the armor plating.

.

"Don't worry, Commander, they fix her good as new".

Turning around, Evan smiled when he saw Vera leaning against her own Echo-class close support warmecha. Dark-haired, bold, reckless, and drop-dead beautiful Vera Kressler. She was a damned good mecha driver too and had the kills to prove it. Evan liked her direct, close-in, no-holds-barred fighting style. Combined with the shattering punch of the scattercannons on her 75-ton Echo she was absolutely fearsome in close combat. She didn't take any prisoners, in love or in war. He remembered how her wingman Chris Gordon had once tried to hit on her and had to be helped to medbay when she kneed him in the groin.

He counted himself fortunate that she had always had a thing for him. At least that was what Jeanne O'Leary, the other female mecha pilot in his squadron had confided to him. Evan found that he was attracted to her too but an intimate relationship was just too much weight to carry around during the campaign. He had kept their relationship friendly, but formal. Evan had been all too aware that he may have had to order her to her death in one of the many desperate battles they had fought.

He watched as she approached him in quick strides, wiping her greasy hands on her BDU pants. She was never one to let the techs handle all the dirty work on her warmecha. Once you got past her beautiful face and superbly-toned body, she was definitely "one of the guys". Vera could swear and debate the merits of filthy jokes with the best of them.

There were several rumors circulating the tech crews that she was lesbian but Evan put it down to ego-repair after their pickup attempts were shot down in flames. Jeanne, her best friend, had reassured him that Vera had a healthy female appreciation for men, especially for her squadron commander, but not before swearing him to secrecy on pain of death. Evan noted that the sweat-stained grey undershirt she wore did not quite hide the enticing swell of her firm breasts.

"I see your mecha has quite a few dents in the fender too," he said.

"You should see the other guy," She laughed.

"You really should get cleaned up for the big celebration tonight"

"Formal parties bore me to death, Sir," Vera wrinkled her nose in mock disgust.

"Everybody will be there. Plus you'll get to watch Chris squirm as I pin that gold gong on him," Evan mentioned.

"He's earned it. It took big ones to stand there in the courtyard entrance holding off three heavies single-handed. Even if his pickup lines suck."

Evan chuckled as she moved closer, her eyes never leaving his face.

"So... do I get dibs on the first dance with the handsome young Duke Frome?" she asked.

Evan grimaced at the mention of his formal title.

"Ugh! I'll never get used to people calling me Duke."

"You should get used to it. As the handsome Duke-savior of Gideon IV, you have lots of neat privileges... like being able to pick from the hordes of young, willing virgins all eager and willing to repay you for their freedom from tyranny..."

"Vera, I wish your jokes were as polished as your piloting skills," Evan said, his face screwing up in disgust.

"Not joking, Commander. At least not about the handsome part, Sir," she countered a wicked grin on her face.

"Kissing up to a superior officer is not really a commendable trait in this army, Sergeant.'

Vera laughed, walking away to work on her mecha again. His eyes followed her, noting the easy, balanced grace in which she moved. A pity those baggy BDU pants hid her legs so completely. He had seen them often enough (although he took great care not to stare) when she showered with the rest of the mecha pilots. Often Evan fantasized about those long, sleek, limbs wrapped around his waist... grinding her hips onto his... her long, dark hair cascading down her shoulders as she moaned in pleasure...

Evan quickly found himself hardening at the carnal thoughts. Startled, he shook himself out of his daydreaming to wave at Vera and the tech crew before departing to finalize the remaining preparations for the night. As he left the hanger he knew she was watching his departing figure. The thought left a smile on his face as he made his way to the main palace building.

THE party celebrations were in full swing as Evan made his rounds, greeting his troops, friends, and the dozens of military and civilian leaders. In the ballroom, the dance floor was a hive of activity as the various couples paired off. Evan chuckled at the sight of Gunny Jimenez with his arm around the delectable waist of the Comms Officer Eliza Irving. Looks like the old grease monkey could still pull the women.

Looking around, he saw Jeanne, all made up and looking absolutely beautiful and Chris, with a huge grin on his boyish features and his left arm in a sling. The two were fairly groping each other, even with Chris's dislocated shoulder. Their friendship had become close over the course of the campaign, and Evan was in no doubt what they were going to do after the party. Why not, Evan thought, they both earned it.

He stopped looking around when the slender figure of Vera Kressler caught hold of his arm, spinning him around. Her unruly dark hair was neatly tucked into a rather severe bun, and she looked gorgeous, even in a dress uniform. She smelt good too. Vera scowled when she noticed him sniffing pointedly.

"With all due respect Commander, tell anybody that I have per-fume on and I will kill you, Sir" she whispered.

"Nothing in the regs against that, Sergeant," he grinned.

Evan allowed her to drag him to the center of the room, a sly smile on her deep burgundy-painted lips. Typical of the direct manner in which she approached everything, Vera quickly made her presence felt. Evan could feel himself get aroused as they danced her breath warm on his cheek. She was not making it any easier for him by rubbing her svelte body against him every chance she got. He could feel her firm breasts press against his chest, her hips grinding into his. Vera kept her eyes locked on his, her unspoken words leaving no doubt what she wanted with him tonight.

Just when Evan thought he would shoot off inside his pants, he breathed in relief as Jeanne cut in on their embrace. She was a fine pilot and it turned out, a great dancer. As he twirled the blonde pilot around, Evan whispered into her ear.

"Take real good care of our hero Chris, Jeanne."

"After tonight, he's gonna get his other arm in a sling too," she grinned.

"Ask Eldrin to show you the guest quarters. Best room in the house. Compliments from the Duke for a job well done."

Jeanne blushed knowingly as she gave him a little squeeze. Evan turned his head to wink at Chris, who was busy enjoying the proximity of one of the several attractive women he would dance with that night. They all wanted to get to know the decorated hero of Gideon.

AFTER several rounds and dancing partners, Evan heard the announcement that the fireworks display were about to begin. Even above the noisy chatter of the crowd, could be heard the first of the fireworks prepared for the night. As part of the crowd left the ballroom, Evan looked around for Vera. He searched for her for some time until frustrated, he left for the balconies upstairs to view the fireworks display. A small crowd was milling around the main upper balcony, chatting animatedly as the massive bursts of light and sound spiraled into the night sky.

As Evan made his way back to the guests, he caught sight of the slim figure of Vera waving to him across the room. She smiled knowingly, wetting her lips with her tongue. Before Evan could call to her, she turned abruptly, heading out of the building. Hurriedly, he followed her. Not slowing, she walked quickly away from the main palace.

In the distance, Evan could make out the darkened shape of the mecha hangers. She appeared to be heading straight for it. He was some 50 meters behind her when she reached the squat building. Evan heard hydraulics hiss as Vera unlocked the massive armored doors to the mecha hangar before disappearing inside. Reaching the doorway, Evan peered inside the cavernous gloom, dimly lit by small lights, meant to preserve the night vision of the pilots.

"Why don't you come on in, Commander?" Vera said from somewhere, a hint of amusement in her voice.

Evan played with the controls, closing the massive doors and shutting out the chill of the night air. Moving around the scattered equipment, he looked around for the dark haired pilot.

"I'm a bit over aged to be playing hide and seek, Sergeant Kressler"

"Up here, Sir."

Looking up he spied the slender figure up on the access gantry beside her favourite mecha. Evan quickly made his way between the stacks of heavy equipment, joining her on the raised platform, some ten meters from the hangar floor.

"And what is the meaning of this, Sergeant?" he asked in a mock authoritarian tone as he stepped onto the platform.

She brought herself to attention, eyes locked on his.

"Sir, permission to speak freely," she requested, her voice formal.

"Granted."

"I have a confession to make. I know it is against the regs and all, but I am madly in love with my commanding officer."

"I see," he said, playing along. "The army frowns on intimate relations between officer and subordinate."

"I know, Sir. But when he looks at me I just melt," she said, reaching up, her fingers beginning to undo the topmost button on the jacket of her dress uniform.

"I tried to suppress the feelings, Sir, but it didn't work," she continued, freeing the second button down, then the third.

"I have these... urges... I fantasize about him every night... and sometimes during the day as well..." she said, as she finally freed the jacket of her dress uniform.

She shrugged her shoulders with a sigh, the discarded garment fluttering to the steel grille flooring. Evan watched in fascination as she went to work on the buttons on her blouse, undoing them ever so slowly. He swallowed as he caught the first glimpses of her smooth, tanned skin between the openings of her blouse. She completed unbuttoning her blouse, pulling it free from her skirt. Evan could see the firm swell of her breasts, confined by the black bra she wore underneath.

"I dream about him holding me... making love to me... when I do myself, I pretend it is him moving deep inside me..."

Shrugging the loosened blouse free of her well-toned shoulders, she let it fall carelessly. Her deft hands moved sensuously downwards, gliding across her flanks and her flat stomach. Eventually, she found the clasp of her dress skirt. With infinite care, she undid the fastenings, dragging the zipper all the way down to her thighs.

"I would do anything for him.... let him take me anywhere... in any position he wanted..."

Evan held his breath as her sleek thighs came into view, tanned, soft and enticing in the dim light. Wriggling her hips wantonly, she let the skirt puddle around her ankles as she stepped out of it. Underneath, she had on a pair of sexy black thong panties which showed her ass to full effect. Evan let his gaze run over those sensuous curves, following her sleek legs all the way to her taut, firm buttocks.

"And most of all..." she breathed, "...I want him to fuck me senseless, until I scream."

It was all too much for the young Duke. Reaching for her, Evan pulled her to him, kissing her hungrily until they both broke off to breathe before going at it again, their tongues working furiously. By the time their mouths parted again, Evan had a raging erection and made haste to get his clothes off as well. She helped him.

Slipping her bra straps off her shoulders, Evan reached behind her to undo her bra, exposing the firm, rounded mounds of her breasts. The nipples were already fully erect in her excitement.

She moaned as she felt his strong hands cup her soft flesh, calloused fingers lightly brushing over the hardened peaks, gasped in pleasure when his mouth enveloped one sensitive nipple, nibbling and licking wetly.

Vera reached up, freeing her long dark hair to spill over her bare shoulders. His cock was rock-hard when she reached down and surrounded it in her small fist.

"Mmmmmm... so big..." she said appreciatively, lowering her mouth on him. Her pink tongue flicked out, tasting the tip of his cock.

"Lie back, Sir. I dreamed about doing this for you..." she whispered "taking you in my mouth, all of it, until you cum..."

She began to lick all the way around his cock, coating it with her saliva as Evan groaned in pleasure at her expert tongue. Leaning forward, she got her lips around his cock, taking as much of the hard length inside her warm, moist mouth as she could manage. Her intense licking and sucking, and her fist pumping on his shaft soon broke Evan's control as he grunted, feeling himself on the verge of a climax.

He tried to warn her he was about to cum, but she ignored him. She held his cock inside her working mouth until the first jets of milky cum shot within her. Vera released him after he spent himself, remnants of his cum dribbling down her delicate chin. She licked her glistening lips sensuously, like a cat drunk on cream.

Incredibly, Evan found that was still hard. Probably because her tanned, luscious, almost naked body was dangling in front of his eager eyes. With one motion, Evan jerked her thong panties down to her sleek thighs. His eyes were drawn to the apex of her mound, and the wetly glistening lips of her flowered-open pussy. Pushing the sodden garment slowly down to her ankles, Vera stepped out of her panties, now totally naked to his hungry eyes. Her eyes bright with desire, she pushed him onto his back, his stiff cock standing upright like a flagpole.

Ever so slowly, she lowered herself on him, one deft hand guiding his hard length to where she wanted it. They both groaned in pleasure as she sat down slightly, his cock pushing between the fleshy lips and entering halfway up into her vaginal passage. With a cry she let herself fall onto his cock, her weight driving the hard length all the way inside her slick, warm tunnel.

Her eyes shut with pleasure, Vera began to move her supple body, raising her hips slightly until his cock almost slipped out of her before falling down again to impale herself. She managed a series of soft cries, grinding her hips against his, lost in the ecstasy of his hard length deeply lodged inside her most sensitive regions. Aroused by the sight of her swaying breasts, Evan levered himself upwards so he could mouth those perfect round orbs.

The combined sensations of his tongue rasping over her painfully hard nipples and the delicious wet frictioning of his cock inside her vaginal passage quickly brought her to the edge of a climax. Crying out, she arched her back in response as she felt her taut muscles began to spasm uncontrollably.

As her vaginal walls contracted around his engorged cock, Evan lost control and came as well, shooting his load inside her. Vera shuddered as she felt his warm juices spurt wildly deep inside her body. He held onto her writhing body as she rode out her orgasm, her hair flying wildly as she tossed her head about. Spent, she collapsed atop him with a gargled cry, her breathing ragged against his sweaty chest, his cock still lodged inside her.

Vera recovered quickly, raising herself off his muscular form. A slow flow of their mingled juices spilled out of her pussy as his deflated cock slid out of her. Evan watched in amusement as the glistening fluids dribbled down her soft thighs, dripping the ten meters down to the hard concrete below. The techs were going have a fun time deducing the source of those stains tomorrow.

Smiling seductively, she crawled on her hands and knees, turning round so that he was facing her firm, rounded buttocks. Vera sighed as she lay her head down on her jacket, raising her hips to present him with a full, unobstructed view of her sex. She knew Evan could see the cum drying on the fleshy lips of her pussy, felt the rivulets of her juices running down her sleek thighs. Evan felt his eyes drawn to the dark crease between her taut buttocks even as she reached behind, pulling her taut buttocks apart.

Vera moaned as she felt his thick, hard length nose about her sex, looking for and finding the engorged lips bordering her sensitive opening. Her hands searched for him, trying to position him to where he could penetrate her. Evan had other ideas however, as he drove himself across the fleshy lips. She gasped at the sudden, sharp pleasure as the tip of him rubbed over her fiercely erect clitoris.

"Yes!" she hissed at the delicious sensations through clenched, perfect white teeth.

Satisfied that he had located the elusive button, her commander began his assault, poling his member across that tiny bud at the apex of her vaginal lips. Her eyes shut, Vera cried out at the intense pleasure as the ribbed ridges of his cock rasped exquisitely over her super-sensitive clit. Again and again, slowly at first, then faster and faster until she clawed at the steel flooring beneath her, wailing out her passion.

Evan held onto her sweaty flanks as she shuddered in a series of violent orgasms, totally consumed by her passion. Vera screamed as her supple body jerked about, the uncontrolled spasms inside her sending a spray of her juices gushing out of her fully aroused pussy. As he felt her fluids drenching his groin, Evan withdrew slightly, sighting on the warm, inviting entrance of her pussy. With a grunt, he mounted her from behind, sinking his well-lubed cock deeply inside her. She cried out, the sudden penetration triggering another climax inside her.

Completely aroused by the delicious feel of the tight, resisting walls of her vaginal passage, Evan plunged himself as far as he could go inside her before withdrawing. Again and again, increasing in tempo until he was slamming his groin against her buttocks, with each thrust eliciting an appreciative moan from Vera. He delighted in the way her breasts quivered so enticingly with each deep stroke. From the sounds she was making, she was finding this assault extremely pleasurable too.

Vera came quickly, her gargled, choking cry announcing her climax. She always enjoyed this position best, being taken from behind. Even as she writhed in her passion, Vera reached back with both hands, parting the globes of her buttocks. She was going to have her deepest, darkest desire fulfilled. She had always wanted to be taken this way, but had never dared to do so. Evan was so engrossed driving himself into her slick pussy that he failed to hear her murmured request. She repeated it.

"...Fuck me in the ass, Commander" she moaned, looking back at him.

She felt Evan pause, uncertain.

"In my ass... but go easy at first..." she begged as she pulled her buttocks apart, fully exposing her pink, winking anus.

Evan did not need a third invitation as he slipped out of her engorged pussy, letting his glistening cock drag across her nether vale. Vera sighed in pleasure as she felt the head of his rock-hard cock nestle in the entrance of her most intimate orifice. She nudged her hips backwards slightly, feeling him press inside her, stretching the tight ring of muscle around her virgin anus. He pushed forward slowly, totally fascinated at the sight of his thick length buried between the taut, sweaty globes of her buttocks, inching its way into her rear passage.

Her perfect white teeth clenched, Vera took several sharp breaths, trying to relax her anal muscles as his cock pressed deeper into her beautiful ass. She gasped at the pain of his entry, even as she reveled in the sheer, exhilarating lewdness of being taken in her forbidden orifice. She clenched his fists powerfully, her knuckles white and her fingers clawing at the steel flooring beneath her. He was halfway inside her already, but she wanted more.

"Oh! Go on!" she cried.

Encouraged, Evan slowly pushed his rampant cock all the way into her anal passage, hilting himself against the rounded globes of her buttocks. He paused momentarily, allowing her to recover, again marveling at the totally arousing sight of his cock lodged deeply inside her ass. As the pain subsided, Vera began to make little cries, thrusting her hips back against him impatiently, eager to have the full experience of anal sex.

Grasping hold of her slim hips, he began to move against her, his cock rubbing exquisitely against the walls of her painfully tight rear passage. She cried out in complete surrender, jerking her hips backwards to meet his thrusts, the incredible combination of pain and pleasure driving all coherent thoughts from her mind.

Totally aroused now, Evan reached forward for her swaying breasts. Vera gasped at the added sensations as he cupped the soft mounds in his hands, locating first one hardened nipple, then the other. Her cries became more vocal, increasing in intensity as she felt her orgasm began to build. She reached back between her lewdly spread apart thighs, searching with one free hand. Her fingers glistened with her own juices as she found the delicate pink bud at the apex of the fleshy lips of her pussy. Vera felt her pleasure double, making her dizzy with lust.

"Fuck me, Sir!" she urged him, "...fuck me in the ass!"

With Vera wailing and screaming in her passion, her supple, writhing body impaled upon his cock, Evan could not hold off much longer. Grunting, he fell atop her, tasting the salty sweat on her bare back, his weight driving his engorged member as far as it would go into her anal passage. A second later, Vera felt his cock pulse, shooting off deep inside her rectum. The feel of his warm fluids splashing inside her brought her to orgasm as well, her back arching, completely overcome with passion.

Evan continued to pump into her ass as he came, expending his entire load inside her. Moving against her tight, warm flesh until at last they collapsed in a sweaty tangle of limbs to the steel flooring of the gantry platform, breathing heavily. Vera moaned in disappointment as he withdrew from her anus, cum seeping out of the pink, winking orifice.

Evan lay atop her prone form for long moments, caressing her gently, enjoying the satiny feel of her soft skin. A sheen of sweat made her body gleam enticingly in the dim light. They fell asleep in the shadow of her hulking warmecha, wrapped in each other's arms.

The End

Here is a sample from another story you may enjoy:

Arne Mellor

Sensational Possession

DEMON LUST I

PARANORMAL EROTICA

As she dried herself after her morning shower, Professor Kathleen Tarrant took note of the small brown package on her table. Delivered to her apartment yesterday while she was out, it was postmarked Alexandria, Egypt. It bore no sender or return address.

Intrigued, she scrabbled at the plain brown wrapping, unveiling a small, ornate book wrapped carefully in a musty-smelling cloth wrap. The cover was of dark leather, faded with age, with brass reinforcement on the spine and corners. A brass clasp shaped like an eagle's talon held the book closed. There were inscriptions engraved deeply into the metal, the words of which she did not recognize. As she examined the strange artifact, she felt a sharp pain and saw blood on her finger. She had pricked herself on a spiny protrusion that didn't seem to have been there before.

Kathleen noticed a drop of her blood on the brass, bright red against the dull, cold metal. As she watched, the red spots slowly shrank to nothingness, as if the book was absorbing it. Drinking it, it seemed. Slightly alarmed, the young professor hurriedly rewrapped the artifact before placing it carefully in a drawer, intending to bring it to her study for a full analysis later.

In the rush of the day, Kathleen forgot all about the book until she was getting ready for bed. She retrieved the book from the drawer, setting it carefully on her desk and turning on the lamp. Slipping on a pair of white cotton gloves, she worked the brass clasp loose, and carefully opened the pages.

As she turned over the aged and yellowed pages, Kathleen marvelled at the flowing Arabic script and regretted not having the least bit of instruction in the language. Her specialty and passion was Europe of the Middle Ages. Still, she knew several colleagues at the University who could probably help her out and resolved to bring the book to work tomorrow.

As she closed the book, she noticed that several of the brass protrusions on the spine and corners could be slid around, or turned, or pushed inward, each one unique. Fascinated, the dark-haired professor put her full attention to examining the metalwork. With a start, she realized that they appeared to be tiny puzzles. After some work with the aid of a magnifier, her skilled fingers solved the tiny puzzles on 4 of the corners, each time being rewarded with a click as the protrusions slid into hidden recesses.

As she studied the final puzzle on the spine, she felt a prickly sensation at the back of her neck. Kathleen hesitated for several moments, until her curiosity won out. With a satisfied smile, she worked the final puzzle. As she heard the click, she felt her skin grow cold suddenly.

She paused, all senses alert, unsure of what she had done. With a terrible rush, she felt something enter her mind, probing her consciousness. A cold and malevolent entity, its intentions alien and unfathomable. Kathleen heard herself scream even as she stumbled, stunned by the suddenness of the psychic attack as she felt the intruder probing her defenseless, protected mind.

And she felt herself falling... falling...

If you enjoyed this sample then look for <u>Sensational Possession</u>.

Also by this Author

About the Author

Arne Mellor has been writing stories since the age of ten. His first literary reviewer was his Biology teacher who caught him writing Conan stories during class. In Arne's day job, he writes excruciatingly detailed technical manuals for financial computer systems. In his free time, he lets his keyboard wander into the realms of history, mythology, science-fiction and erotica. He currently resides in a tiny East Asian country more famous for sinful food than sinful passions.

From the Author

Check my page on Amazon and my blog for Updates and interesting info.

Author Central - http://www.amazon.com/Arne-Mellor/e/B00A75W1PA
Author Blog - http://arne-mellor.awesomeauthors.org/

If you enjoyed any of my books then please share the love and click like on my books in Amazon.

If you write me a review and send me an email I will send you a free book, or many.
(Just know that these emails are filtered by my publisher.)

Good news is always welcome.

One Last Thing, For Kindle Readers...

When you turn the page, Kindle will give you the opportunity to rate this book and share your thoughts on Facebook and Twitter. If you enjoyed my writings, would you please take a few seconds to let your friends know about it? Because... when they enjoy they will be grateful to you and so will I.

Thank You!

Arne Mellor
arne_mellor@awesomeauthors.org

www.ingramcontent.com/pod-product-compliance
Lightning Source LLC
Chambersburg PA
CBHW071355130626
46556CB00005B/2203